THIS WALKER BOOK BELONGS TO:

_____

_____

_____

for
Patrick

First published 2004 by Walker Books Ltd
87 Vauxhall Walk, London SE11 5HJ

This edition published 2005

2 4 6 8 10 9 7 5 3 1

© 2004 Clare Jarrett

The right of Clare Jarrett to be identified as
author/illustrator of this work has been asserted by her in
accordance with the Copyright, Designs and Patents Act 1988

This book has been typeset in Aunt Mildred

Printed in China

British Library Cataloguing in Publication Data:
a catalogue record for this book is available
from the British Library

ISBN 1-84428-553-7

www.walkerbooks.co.uk

The Best Picnic Ever

Clare Jarrett

WALKER BOOKS
AND SUBSIDIARIES
LONDON • BOSTON • SYDNEY • AUCKLAND

One day Jack went to the park
with his mum to have a picnic.
While Mum made the picnic,
Jack looked about.

"I wish there was someone to play with," said Jack.

"There is," said
Giraffe. "Me!"

"Please come to our picnic," said Jack.
"How kind," said Giraffe, "but
first let's play."

"We'll gallop," said Giraffe.
"And whiz and whoosh," said Jack.
And while Mum made the picnic,

Jack and Giraffe went
gallopy, gallopy, gallopy through
the tall grass.

Then they met Elephant.
"That looks fun," he said.

"Come to our picnic," said Jack.
"How kind," said Elephant,
"but first let's play."

"Let's trumpet,"
said Elephant.
"And make a huge noise," said Jack.
And while Mum made the picnic,
Jack and Elephant went toot, toot,
toot, tootley-toot-toot, with Giraffe
going gallopy, gallopy, gallopy
through the tall grass behind them.

Then they met Leopard.
"What a great noise,"
he said.

"Come and join our picnic," said Jack.
"How kind," said Leopard,
"but first can we play?"

"Let's leap about," said Leopard.
"Great long lolloping leaps," said Jack.
And while Mum made the picnic,
Jack and Leopard went lollopy,

lollopy, lollopy, with Elephant going
toot, toot, toot, tootley-toot-toot and
Giraffe going gallopy, gallopy, gallopy
through the tall grass behind them.

Then they met Tiger.
"Come to our picnic,"
said Jack.
"How kind,"
said Tiger,
"but first
let's dance."

"And tap our toes," said Jack.
And while Jack and Tiger danced,
Leopard went lollopy, lollopy, lollopy
and Elephant went toot, toot, toot,
tootley-toot-toot and Giraffe went
gallopy, gallopy, gallopy behind them.
They tapped and lolloped and tooted
and galloped, faster and faster,
until they heard Mum say ...

"The picnic's ready!"

"Hurrah!" said everyone.

So they all went back to the
most delicious picnic.

There were sausages, pizza,
chocolate cake and strawberries.

Soon it was time to go home.
"Goodbye," said all the animals.
"Goodbye," said Jack. "And thank you,
everyone. That was the

best picnic ever!"

WALKER BOOKS is the world's leading
independent publisher of children's books.
Working with the best authors and illustrators
we create books for all ages, from babies
to teenagers – books your child will
grow up with and always remember. So…

FOR THE BEST CHILDREN'S BOOKS,
LOOK FOR THE BEAR